THREE WAYS TO DIE

CASE FILES: POCKET-SIZED MURDER MYSTERIES

RACHEL AMPHLETT

THREE WAYS TO DIE

ONE

The second time Xander MacKenzie loaded the AWM-F rifle, it was a stifling Wednesday morning in Corpus Christi, Texas.

Sweat trickled from his shaved hairline to his shirt collar, pooling in the armpits of the white cotton shirt he found on a secondhand rack the day before. The cuffs were missing a button or two but no matter--the sleeves were rolled up to his elbows, and the suit pants passed for well-worn rather than threadbare, so long as he didn't peer too closely at the shiny material on the knees.

A black canvas backpack lay at his feet, the familiar white sports logo on the top flap obscured by the frantic scribbles of a marker pen at six-thirty that morning, moments after Xander had killed the alarm on his phone two minutes before it was due to go off.

He hadn't slept well.

Hadn't for the past three nights, not since the last time.

Beside the backpack, a half-empty takeaway coffee cup was beginning to sag, the cardboard looking tired.

He picked it up, took a sip of the insipid local excuse for Arabica beans, and grimaced as the hot liquid scalded his empty stomach.

At least the caffeine whacked him between the eyes.

That was all that mattered right now.

He drained the drink, scrunched up the cup and shoved it into the backpack, then thumbed five .300 Winchester rounds into the detachable magazine, a faint metallic click emanating from the clip as each found its rightful place.

A pinky blue tinged the hazy horizon, and there was a stillness in the air that promised another humidity-soaked day that would do little to slick away the remnant stink of exhaust fumes wafting up from the street below.

Somewhere down there, thirty floors beneath his splayed feet, someone started to fry bacon, the fatty aroma cloying with the sticky sweet scent of maple syrup.

Bastards.

Slapping the magazine into place, Xander exhaled, calming his heart rate and fighting the adrenaline that surged through his veins.

He had missed this if he were honest.

The planning.

The chase.

The kill.

He had been out of action for fourteen months

after an unfortunate incident in Hungary that was kept out of the newspapers but ended his special forces career, and then, just as he was starting to get established in the private sector and his reputation was becoming cemented amongst the dark web community where he lurked, that fucking plague came along.

It had taken all his nefarious skills and the past year to claw his way back to a point where he could comfortably pay the bills without resorting to laboring or bartending, especially as he wasn't the only one vying for work.

And he hated manual labor.

Hated dirt on his hands, which was why, unlike some of his peers, he refused to use any alternatives to a firearm, including knives.

Even poison was messy, especially if the dose was wrong.

His lip curled in a snarl as he recalled the client's words that first time they spoke over an encrypted call, the implication that there were cheaper, better alternatives to his services.

Except that none of the pros was taking bookings for at least another three months, and this job was urgent.

So it was his.

A deep inhalation--ignoring the bacon and maple syrup--another exhale, and Xander dropped to his knees behind the concrete parapet, his gaze turning to the busy intersection criss-crossing the finance district below.

The building was half residential, half

commercial with the lower twenty floors dedicated to office space.

Beside him, the building's enormous air conditioning units rumbled and strained to deliver relief set at precisely seventy-two degrees Fahrenheit to the occupants, a mixture of actuaries, bankers, stock-brokers--as well as a seasoned in-house legal team who worked tirelessly to stop the rest of them doing something stupid enough to get arrested.

He flexed his fingers within the nitrile gloves, his skin already overheating from the protective layer between his hands and the weapon, then lowered his head and peered through the telescopic sight, his guts giving an involuntary twist at the sudden change in focus.

Tracking the muzzle a little to the left, he found the spot beside the coffee wagon, the place where the target had been standing every morning for the past three days at precisely a quarter after nine to order his double shot cappuccino with chocolate flakes.

An abomination to behold.

The target wasn't much better to look at, either.

Lawrence Afflan was a large man in his late fifties.

He carried his weight across a belly that overlapped his pants belt by several inches and over three chins that spilled from his shirt collar. Average height, thinning hair--and with sole direct access to a large sum of money spread across four separate bank accounts in three different countries.

Money that had been taken from the client through a series of administrative forfeitures, civil foreclosures and the like.

Money the client now wanted back.

And by the end of the month before the big one, a court case that would see the client facing criminal charges and with it, the forfeit of his remaining assets.

Xander snorted.

By now, he should have been on a beach somewhere in the South Pacific.

Instead, here he was, sweltering under a Texas summer sun, hoping to hell it went right this time.

Because there had been an earlier attempt on Lawrence Afflan's life, just four days ago.

It happened like this…

TWO

Four days ago

Lawrence Afflan shovelled a handful of freshly unwrapped soft mints into his mouth, salivating.

He could still taste the bitter afterburner of the office manager's excuse for filter coffee. It clung to the insides of his cheeks, slaked the skin under his tongue, and--for some inexplicable reason known only to biologists--seemed determined to hang onto the fine hairs that protruded from his left nostril.

His teeth found the chewy centre of the mints, mashing them to a pulp while his fingers drummed the worn leather cover of his notebook.

An air conditioning vent rumbled above his head, a white noise that thrummed its way across his scalp and burrowed into his thoughts, the cool air seducing the gathered delegates into a lethargic relief from the temperatures outside.

It did nothing to dispel the stink from the filter coffee urn that sat sentinel on an oak sideboard on the far side of the room though, a red light near the top of the stainless steel drum winking at him.

A mock art deco clock on the wall above it ticked the seconds by, its sonorous notes fine-tuned by a group of lab rats somewhere in Los Gatos, according to the woman from procurement.

Or so the rumour went.

Lawrence tore his gaze away from the minute hand as it dragged its way around for another circuit, and forced himself to concentrate as his tongue found the last remains of mint.

Across the oval-shaped mahogany conference table that had once been polished to a high sheen and now resembled a war zone of scrunched up sticky notes and discarded meeting agendas, a young analyst fresh out of college and even fresher between the ears was rambling through a list of outstanding priorities.

A list that had grown exponentially since the woman joined them last week.

Mary McDeaver, twenty-four years old, flame haired with a sprinkle of freckles across her nose and cheeks and--according to the man who introduced her to the team--shoe-horned into a temporary administrative role by a personnel department hell-bent on spending the last cent of their budget before it was taken away.

Within days, she was snapped up by the case manager for the duration of the trial.

What she lacked in knowledge she made up for

in an almost puppy-like eagerness to learn--including finding out how to source his favourite candy, which even impressed the woman from procurement.

Lawrence flicked away the empty mint wrappers and wearily pinched his nose, closing his eyes.

The college grad tripped over her words, stumbled into the next paragraph and then skidded to a halt.

Conversation around the table faltered.

"Sir?" a man's voice ventured.

Lawrence sighed and raised his gaze. "Benji, how much time has your team had to cross-check the prosecution's statements?"

"Erm, two months, sir."

"So why am I only hearing about these matters now?" He dropped his paw of a hand to the table with a bang.

Mary, to her credit, didn't flinch, and instead turned her gaze to the case manager, arching an eyebrow.

A faint blush crept above Benji's shirt collar. "It was an unfortunate oversight, but I've already tasked two teams in the past twenty-four hours to look into it. I should have an update by close of business today."

Lawrence glared at him for a fraction of a second longer, then lowered his eyes to the scrawled note at the top of his notebook, the letters encircled by red felt pen circles. "And how are the outstanding matters proceeding concerning Mr Bingham's finances?"

Benji waved his hand towards Mary. "I believe you were tasked with that?"

"I was," she said, squaring her shoulders before shooting a smile at Lawerence. "The District Attorney's office signed off the authorisations at eight this morning. They were served at the bank fifteen minutes later, and our cyber team is currently analysing the data. Specifically, I've requested them to concentrate on the two weeks either side of the shipments into Galveston that we believe are the primary objective."

Lawrence tried and failed to contain a smirk as Benji's shoulders dropped, the attempted deflection at blame failing spectacularly.

"Good," he said, pushing back his chair and gathering his notes. "Then we'll reconvene at two for an update."

Benji's eyes widened as he made for the door. "Sir? Sir, where are you going?"

"To find a proper fucking coffee," Lawrence growled.

———

Xander swung the baseball cap round back to front and raised the binoculars.

Along the River Walk far below, tourists and locals clamoured the concrete path that meandered alongside the San Antonio waterway.

Cafés and restaurants spilled their guts onto the sidewalk, a clutter of tables and chairs positioned invitingly, tempting passers-by to stop and rest under brightly coloured awnings, many with familiar franchise logos emblazoned across the front.

A band was tuning up somewhere, all brass and drums and cymbals, a mush of noise that clamoured back and forth on a gentle warm wind that caressed the fine hairs on his bare forearms.

It was a twenty minute drive from the FBI's local offices, but here was where Lawrence Afflan had established his hand-picked team of investigators for the biggest trial in Texas history, and so here was where the client wanted the shot taken.

Send them a signal, he'd said.

Xander lowered the binoculars, his gaze falling to the weapon laid out beside him.

The rifle was a SAKO TRG 42, and when he met the client's contact at a disused tire warehouse south of the city to collect it, he knew straight away there would be a problem.

It was the client's choice of rifle--and the client evidently knew nothing about rifles.

For a start, the SAKO was way down the list of preferred sniper rifles, much lower than the other two Xander had requested.

Second, the client had provided a suppressor and insisted it be used.

No matter that the suppressor would affect the trajectory and accuracy of the shot.

No matter that by the time Afflan appeared, the band would be in full swing, obliterating any indication of where the fatal shot originated from, rendering any suppressor useless in the circumstances.

But…

This was the first job in too long, and Xander was in no mood to argue.

He just wanted the money.

Lowering the binoculars, he shouldered the rifle into position, splaying his legs behind him to balance that and his body weight and rested the barrel on a sports towel he'd laid upon the concrete parapet.

Eye to the scope, he tracked back and forth along the River Walk, sighting on random strangers to test the accuracy of the range finder, then eased away for a moment and checked his watch.

Two minutes.

According to the client's sources, Afflan's caffeine addiction would see him outside by nine fifteen, give or take thirty seconds.

Xander could feel his heart rate starting to churn, and cursed under his breath.

He was out of practice.

Recalling the breathing exercises he had used while he was in the special forces unit, he settled back to the scope and counted.

Four in.

Hold for four.

Four out.

Hold for four.

Repeat.

Ad nauseam.

He found the entry door to the investigator's offices easily.

It was the one dressed up to look like one of the gift stores elbowing for space amongst the cafés, the ones with the same foreign-manufactured tasteless trinkets that were sold in a million other stores between here and Austin. Except this particular one had no back office, no stock room, and no loading dock at the rear.

Instead, a staircase led off from the permanently closed women's changing room, thirteen steps that were barricaded by a reinforced steel door guarded by two Federal agents, who were armed to the teeth.

Infiltrating the building had been deemed impossible, at least at this short notice, at least if any chance of success was expected.

Xander's heart rate calmed, his muscles relaxing into the rifle, his forefinger resting gently on the trigger guard until it was required.

His breathing steadied as a familiar figure appeared at the doorway to the gift shop, a brace of hangers-on in his wake, both wearing the obligatory wraparound sunglasses.

The man in a navy suit and pale blue tie to the left of Afflan was Benji Hazlitt, an ambitious senior analyst who the client suspected might take the old man's place once the dust had settled.

The woman on his right was new--young, too--

and seemed eager to impress, the way she was gesticulating while Afflan stalked ahead, his hand raised to silence her.

Two more men hurried after the group, dark suits marking them as standard security detail amongst the brightly clothed tourists.

On cue, the band struck up a jaunty rendition of *The Stars And Stripes Forever*, the swish and sway of the music carrying up to Xander's perch.

It washed over him, as did the indignant squawk of a gull who momentarily paused on the concrete sill before swooping off across the looping watercourse.

His focus honed in on the one man who would earn him thirty thousand dollars in the next few seconds.

The scope's crosshairs were on Afflan's chest, right on the spot where the left lapel of his single-breasted jacket flapped open as the man's swinging gait carried him towards the one place that would seal his fate: the russet-coloured coffee cart on the sidewalk's junction with the sweeping parkland beyond.

Xander's forefinger caressed the trigger.

Bracing himself, he exhaled.

Then fired.

The round exploded from the muzzle, the suppressor creating a microscopic wobble in the trajectory.

Afflan ducked.

Confused, Xander flung the rifle to one side and picked up the binoculars, honing in on the panicked crowd who, having cringed and dropped to the sidewalk, were now rushing like wildebeest from a croc attack towards the exits.

Afflan remained crouched, the man's hands to his shoes, his brow furrowed while his gaze scanned the buildings around him.

He was ignoring the pleas from his security detail to return to the building, confusion etched into his face while those around him were fearful.

Sirens were wailing now, closing the distance between Xander and escape.

He sighed, glared at the rifle, then folded the stock, pulled out the spent magazine and shoved it into the black canvas backpack at his feet.

Pulling out his cell phone as he crawled across to the service exit, he dialled one number from memory and bit his lip as the call went through.

"Is it done?"

"He's still alive."

Xander took the stairs two at a time, explaining the problem with the suppressor, the trajectory, the target crouching to tie his shoelace at the exact moment he'd pulled the trigger, and…

The client was furious.

After all, the fee had been paid.

The clock was ticking.

And so, the second attempt was planned.

THREE

Now

Xander flexed his fingers, rolled his neck and arched his back.

Anything to lose the tension.

And the memory of that last debacle.

He scratched at the stubble lining his jaw, ignoring the prickle of sweat between his shoulder blades, and contemplated the scene below once more.

The Corpus Christi business district was swelling now as the suburbs emptied into it, the passive-aggressive honk and shove of rush-hour climaxing before the day's ninth hour.

The intersection was one of the main crossroads in the finance district, a mixture of delivery trucks bearing familiar online retailers' logos, FedEx and DHL mingling with sleek black sedans and white taxis.

An elongated gas-fuelled bus glided to a halt at the stop opposite his position before ejecting a steady stream of commuters that scurried along the sidewalk before disappearing into doorways and covered porticos for another day of... whatever.

Xander snorted, wrinkled his nose disdainfully, and turned his attention back to the coffee wagon on the other side of the junction.

Trade was slowing now as most administrative staff and the like began to seep towards another inevitable day of boredom tinged with ever-increasing frustration, wilting as the temperature continued to climb.

And then, it was over.

Not quite silence, but not the assault of noise there had once been mere minutes ago either.

The air conditioning unit beside him ramped up another gear, a white noise that swept over him and away across the rooftop, and he lowered his eye to the sight.

The rifle's metal sheathing felt familiar under his touch despite the protective gloves. Its shape, form and weight had been something of a comfort during those long nights on duty a lifetime ago and now served as a reminder that this was where he belonged.

This was what he was good at.

He frowned.

Until four days ago, anyway.

He lifted his chin, blinked away the thought, and settled once more.

He was ready for Lawrence Afflan this time.

Any minute now…

FOUR

Lawrence Afflan manoeuvred his enormous bulk through the steel turnstile that barred entry to the outside world, edging sideways while eyeing the security team that patrolled the temporary field office.

A high sheen sparkled off the floor that squeaked under his soles as he shuffled forward, the tiles capturing the morning sunlight penetrating the bullet-proof glass front doors before it met an untimely death on the beige plaster walls.

Once through the gate, he glared at the stumpy young guard who handed back his weapon and wallet, daring him to smirk while Afflan straightened his jacket. Then he glanced over his shoulder as the guard's gaze shifted to where Mary blithely strolled through the turnstile in his wake, her eager stride only amplified by the determined look in her eyes.

"Benji says you shouldn't be doing this, sir. He's concerned you might…"

"Benji needs to relax. There's been no chatter from our sources to suggest Bingham will make another attempt on my life, not so soon. Besides, two teams are watching his place in West Lake Hills. No one's gone in or out of there in the past forty-eight hours, and there's been nothing on the wire taps either."

An audible sigh escaped Mary's lips as she took back her purse with a smile of thanks from the guard. "Sir, we can't be sure of that, can we?"

He watched while she holstered her weapon, flipped her hair over the collar of her navy blazer, and then angled her jaw so it was a little shy of petulance.

"Sir, if something happens to you, it's my career on the line."

A loud bellow of laughter escaped him, echoing off the walls and turning heads their way. "Good to know you've got your priorities right, Miss McDeaver."

"I didn't mean it like that, sir. I…"

He waved away her apology, already heading to the exit. "I know. Right, where's that security detail?"

Two agents emerged from behind the faux marble reception desk that swept the width of the atrium, descending on them with a swiftness honed with experience.

"Sir, the Director called," said the taller of the two. "He needs you in his office at oh nine thirty."

Afflan checked his watch. "There's still time for coffee."

———

Running a finger under his shirt collar and squinting across the intersection, Afflan rued his hastiness and silently cursed both the young analyst at his elbow and the two security men for their foresight in remembering to wear sunglasses.

It was almost the end of June, and there was still no respite from the heatwave that had gripped the state since Memorial Day weekend.

If it wasn't for the weapon tucked into the holster under his arm, he wouldn't have worn the jacket but despite an open carry licence, he didn't want to draw attention to himself.

Despite his assurances to Mary, despite his nonchalance back there at the security gates, he was worried.

Worried, because the Bureau had known Bingham was ruthless, possibly sociopathic.

But San Antonio had been a lucky break.

He evidently wasn't meant to leave that city alive, and yet here he was, actively pursuing an investigation and chasing another man's millions.

An investigation that could well cost him his life one way or another.

And he was succumbing to a caffeine habit that could contribute to his death, whether by bullet or high blood pressure.

The crosswalk lights turned green and he led the way, lip curling while sweat pooled under his arms. He emitted a relieved sigh when his shoes found the sidewalk once more and he slipped into the welcome shade from the buildings that towered above.

The queue for the coffee cart had dissipated, leaving the owner of it wiping down the counter as they approached.

A burgundy nylon awning stretched out from a wide hatch cut into the side of the cart, and the smell of freshly roasted beans sent Afflan's taste buds somersaulting.

The owner whistled along to the radio while he worked, the song a popular Rolling Stones number from the early seventies that argued with the coffee grinder, then aimed a cheeky wink at Mary McDeaver, even though he was surely old enough to be her grandfather.

"Morning. Beautiful day." He scrunched up the rag and pushed it to one side, then leaned forward and rested his gnarled hands on the sill. "What can I get you?"

"What'll you have?" Afflan said, turning to Benji's young protégé. "I'm buying."

"Oh. Thank you. Um, I'll have a skinny cappuccino please."

Afflan ignored the security detail and turned back to the cart. "And I'll have a double shot cappuccino with chocolate flakes."

The owner wrinkled his nose. "That's a new one."

"Get used to it. I'll be having the same tomorrow." Afflan paid, then glanced over his shoulder to where a decorative fountain splashed recycled water, the droplets sparkling as they fell.

"Come on, we'll sit over there while we're waiting."

Mary shrugged off her blazer and folded it over her arm before trotting after him. "Sir, I think it might be prudent in the circumstances to… oh— '

She stumbled against him, crying out as her heel caught in a crack in the pavers.

Afflan staggered, losing his balance while he reached out to stop her from falling.

Then the fountain head exploded.

Shards of granite flew up into the air before descending across the sidewalk like armoured confetti.

A split second later, there was a fiery *crack* in the air, the report echoing off the glass and concrete structures around them.

The two security men swivelled and crouched as one, weapons drawn while their faces scanned the buildings opposite, each barking commands into their lapel mics.

Screams filled the air, muffled by the persistent ringing in Afflan's ears.

And then Mary was pulling his arm, trying to drag him up from the ground, yelling at him to run, run, run.

FIVE

Xander MacKenzie raced down the service stairs two at a time, the canvas backpack lolling against his shoulder with the weight of the rifle.

It had taken him mere seconds to collect the spent cartridge, fold the stock, rip out the magazine and stow the lot before sprinting across the rooftop, the sound of honking horns and screams billowing up from the intersection below.

His legs were on autopilot, his body pivoting at each landing to leap down the first three steps, a mixture of finely-honed cardio fitness from days in the gym and pure animal instinct.

He couldn't believe Afflan's luck.

Or his own.

Cursing under his breath, he slowed as he reached the twenty-third level, popped open the fire exit door and peered into the hallway beyond.

All the doors to the residential part of the building were closed, save for one at the far end near the elevators.

An elderly lady in her eighties peered at him from behind beer-bottle glasses, her brow furrowed as she blocked his way.

"What's going on?" she barked, clutching an evil-looking tabby cat to her substantial chest. "I heard a gun."

Xander shrugged as he drew closer. "I thought it was a car back-firing, ma'am."

"I can hear screaming," she said. Her eyes narrowed. "I don't know you, do I?"

"I'm on the twenty-fifth. The elevator's stuck so I took the stairs."

"Oh." She stood to one side to let him pass, then called after him. "You should report it to that piece of shit janitor they call a receptionist downstairs."

"I will, thank you, ma'am."

Xander stabbed his finger to the call button, exhaling as the elevator door slid open, and stepped inside.

Dropping the backpack to his feet, he stripped off his T-shirt, pulled out a freshly wrapped white cotton shirt from a side pocket of the bag and tugged it on.

His jeans were next.

By the time he walked out of the elevator, he resembled any one of the smartly-dressed men loitering in the lobby while craning their necks to see what was happening beyond the glass doors.

"What happened?" Xander asked a passing woman, her face pale. "What's going on?"

"Someone said there's a sniper," she managed. "There was gunfire. Didn't you hear it?"

He gave her an apologetic smile. "I was taking a video call with my headphones on. Are the police out there yet?"

"On the intersection, next to where that coffee cart is parked by the fountain."

"I'm sure they'll have the place secured in no time."

She didn't look convinced but turned away from him when someone across the lobby called to her.

Xander spun on his heel and headed for the back door, his phone out, his thumb already pressing the speed dial.

Hurrying now, the need for escape overriding any frustration, he pushed through a service door and out into an alley that ran parallel to the building.

Farther along, it dog-legged past overflowing trash bins before widening as he approached the street beyond.

He could see a patrol car parked skewed to the kerb, lights flashing, a radio squawking at volume while two officers stood next to the open trunk, pulling out rifles and body armour.

The phone was answered after the fourth ring. "What happened?"

"It was bad luck, that's all," Xander began, keeping his voice low as he passed the officers, giving the shorter of the two what he hoped was a respectful nod. He forced himself to stay calm, breathe, and walk. "Send a car to come and get me where we arranged. We'll have to try again. Perhaps in a week, maybe—"

The phone went dead.

"Sonofabitch!"

He froze on the sidewalk, staring at the screen, jaw clenched.

Then his survival instinct kicked in.

The one honed from all those tours in the mountains far, far away from here.

The one that had saved his life.

More than once.

Throwing a quick glance over his shoulder, he spotted the two officers with their backs to him, leaning their weight against their vehicle, legs splayed and rifles propped on the roof while they awaited orders.

A small crowd of onlookers gawped at the intersection from behind hastily erected barriers, any regard for their own safety swiftly swayed by the growing presence of television broadcast vans and eager reporters.

No one looked his way.

Xander turned and stepped off the kerb.

He didn't see the sleek black saloon that hit him.

It scooped him up, breaking his legs as it tumbled him over its hood, his skull smacking the windshield with a sickening thud, and then spat him onto the asphalt in a tangled mess of blood and bone.

Benji Hazlitt's hands froze on the steering

wheel, his jaw slack while he stared at the blood-streaked windshield.

Then his gaze moved to the crumpled form in the middle of the road.

He blinked.

"Shit."

SIX

"So let me get this straight, you killed my would-be assassin with your front fender?"

"Strictly speaking sir, it was the windshield that finished him off. He bounced off the hood and hit his head against the glass."

Afflan raised an eyebrow while his chief analyst shifted from foot to foot. "It's reinforced to withstand a fusillade of bullets, so I'm not surprised."

The two men turned back to the vehicle, its driver's door wide open and the sizeable form of one of the Bureau's top accident investigators leaning inside to take photographs of the dashboard.

Then Benji's phone rang and Afflan watched as he glowered at the screen before answering, then turned away to take the call.

"Are you all right?"

He smiled as Mary sidled between two hastily erected barriers and hurried towards him.

"I am, thanks to you Miss McDeaver. You appear to be my lucky charm."

She blushed at that, then frowned while Benji finished his call and stalked across to one of his men, his voice raised but inaudible amongst the throng of emergency services and Bureau personnel that crowded the sidewalks and road. "Is he okay?"

"He will be." Afflan jerked his chin at the sprawled form on the ground. "Does anyone know who he is?"

"Not yet. We're working on it, although—"

She broke off as Benji returned, straightening his hair and smoothing down his tie.

"That was Headquarters on the phone, sir."

"Oh?" Afflan raised his eyebrows. "Why didn't they phone me?"

Benji shrugged. "Said they couldn't get through. The Director wants me to take one of the pool cars and get you over to a safe house that's been organised north of the city. First thing tomorrow, they're flying you to Atlanta to continue the investigation from there."

"Atlanta?" Afflan choked out a laugh. "I can't run things from Atlanta. What the hell is he thinking?"

"I'm sorry, sir. I didn't ask. I'm just passing on the message." Benji jangled a fresh set of keys in his hand. "If you're ready?"

"Are you okay to drive, after…" Mary looked at the dead man, who was now being manoeuvred into a shiny black body bag by two junior forensic technicians. "I mean, I can if you want…"

Afflan watched as Benji's jaw clenched, and then the man tossed the keys to the young analyst. "Hell, why not? I can check emails on the way."

———

Thirty minutes later, Mary pulled into the driveway of a nondescript suburban property with a white picket fence and a tidy garden.

The front lawn was a lush green bordered by freshly pruned shrubs and bright perennial flowers that stood tall and proud. The porch was painted a fashionable pale gray and a rolled-up newspaper lay on the top of the top step of the stoop.

A stars and stripes flew proudly from a flagpole in the front yard.

"Well this isn't exactly low key, is it?" Afflan grumbled. "May as well have a sign out front saying 'FBI Safe House'."

"It belongs to a military family currently based out in the Gulf, sir," said Benji. "Or so my intel suggests."

"Your intel needs to sort their shit out. Jesus, what happened to flea-bitten apartments and motel rooms?"

"Sounds very twentieth century to me, sir."

Afflan craned his neck to look at Benji in the back seat, but the man had his face lowered to his phone. "When you've served as long as I have…"

"Oh, the garage door's opening," Mary said.

"It's automatic. It's set to recognise the licence plate," came Benji's reply.

"Definitely not twentieth century," Afflan murmured.

He fell silent while Mary eased the car into the darkened maw of the garage and switched off the engine. The door began to close, and as he climbed out and stretched his legs, a series of recessed spotlights in the ceiling blinked to life.

The rumbling of the door mechanism finally stopped, obliterating the last chink of daylight as the galvanised steel met concrete, and Afflan turned his attention to the rear of the garage.

It was larger than he thought, with ample space beyond the vehicle's fender for a heavy-duty workshop bench along the far wall and a dusty multi-gym in one corner.

He noticed with a wry smile that all the tools were in their proper place in racks above the bench, and things like spare nails, screws and bolts were kept in large pickle jars in a neat line below the racks.

Just like he'd expect a Marine corpsman's garage to be.

Except for the dusty multi-gym.

He crossed to it, his brow furrowing as his gaze swept over the steel key stuck midway down the stack of weighted plates rather than left on top.

No corpsman in his experience would leave weights like that.

Afflan's shoe scuffed the side of the padded training bench, his toe finding something heavy before a two pound dumbbell rolled from underneath it.

Frowning, he opened his mouth.

The wisecrack froze on his lips at the simultaneous sound of a bullet being chambered and a gasp from Mary.

"Sorry it's come to this, sir."

He turned to see Benji's arm raised, the barrel of a non-issued revolver pointing right at him. "What's going on?"

"Call it Plan B." The senior analyst side-eyed Mary. "If you move, your boss dies, got it?"

She nodded, eyes wide like a deer caught in headlights while she slowly held up her hands.

Satisfied, Benji turned back to him. "If that idiot had done his job right, you'd have been dead days ago."

"San Antonio?" Afflan snorted. "Where the hell d'you find him, the county fair or something?"

"I had nothing to do with his recruitment."

"So, you're on Bingham's payroll as well, eh?" Shaking his head in wonder, Afflan caught movement beside Benji but kept his gaze firmly on the man and swallowed. "Is it worth trying to talk you out of this?"

Something flickered behind Benji's eyes then.

Regret, perhaps.

Or resolve.

"Not really, sir. I have my orders."

"How much is he paying you?"

Benji's mouth quirked. "Enough."

"Even though you killed his pet assassin?"

"*Because* I killed his pet assassin. So you couldn't find him and question him."

"If you put down the gun, we can sort this out," Afflan persisted, hearing the desperation in his voice.

"He'll never stop. Not until he has his money or you're dead. So I may as well collect the reward myself." There was a smugness to the man's voice now, but Afflan saw the way the revolver wavered.

Just a tiny amount, but it was all she needed.

In one fluid movement, Mary MacDeaver reached under her exquisitely tailored blazer, pulled out her service pistol and shot Benji in the ribcage.

He hit the concrete like a sack of mouldy potatoes.

Then his head exploded, brains and bone splattering across the pitted concrete floor.

Afflan glanced down at his shoes, then grimaced and took a step back.

In the deafening silence that followed, he heard a gulping breath and looked over his shoulder. "Not bad for a junior analyst, Miss McDeaver. And you didn't learn to double tap like that at the Academy, did you?"

She gave a shy smile, her hand steady as she lowered the 9mm Glock. "My pop used to take me hunting, sir. I never miss."

SEVEN

Pushing past a surly group of reporters and TV crew outside his office in downtown Corpus Christi, Afflan glared at a familiar journalist, ignored the microphone thrust under his nose and shoved his way into the foyer.

"Sir, we're ready for you in the conference room," gushed a man in a pale gray suit who joined him at the security turnstile. He peered down his nose at Mary. "Will your assistant be joining us?"

"This young lady just saved my life," snapped Afflan. "And for the third time this week. Of course she's joining us."

They marched into the elevator, the ride up to the thirtieth floor filled with a stony silence while Afflan chewed his lip, his brow furrowed.

Moments later, they were ushered into a large conference room with bare walls except for a large television fixed to one and a photograph of the latest President of the United States of America on the other.

Afflan gave the photograph a cursory glance as he passed beneath it, wondering if the latest incumbent realised just exactly how much danger the people who gave up their lives to serve faced each and every day.

His gaze found Mary, and he gave her a reassuring smile, then stalked around the highly polished mahogany oval table to the windows overlooking a hazy skyline, the city suburbs stretching out beyond the city as far as he could see.

Somewhere out there, Bingham was plotting his demise.

But who would he send next?

Another mercenary?

Another one of Afflan's own team?

He turned and surveyed the room as a surly group of worried-looking senior analysts and case officers filtered through the door, each of them taking one look at the empty chair at the far end of the table and scurrying to other seats instead.

Afflan grimaced and patted his chest.

"Everything okay, sir?" murmured Mary. "You look pale."

"Heartburn." He shrugged. "And don't tell me caffeine doesn't help, you'll sound like my first wife."

"And I'll bet you haven't eaten anything all morning. That won't help, you know." Mary reached into her bag, pulled out a handful of mints and passed them over with a shy smile. "These are all I've got, I'm afraid. I usually carry around a cereal bar or something, but…"

"You're an angel," said Lawrence, already unwrapping the first mint. He turned to the room and raised his voice. "Right, where the hell's the person leading this meeting? I want to know what the hell is going on with local law enforcement and where Bingham is. I want his lawyer on the phone in five minutes. That man's got some explaining to do."

Four of the analysts leapt from their seats, faces flushed while they hurried from the room.

"Do you think Benji was telling the truth?" said Mary while an administrative assistant passed around a meeting agenda. "Do you think Bingham's behind these attempts on your life?"

Lawrence finished chewing, his hand automatically seeking out the next candy. "You joined us after the first attempt in Houston."

"Someone tried to shoot you there?"

"No." Lawrence swallowed. "They've escalated since then. Made it more personal. In Houston, somebody tried to sabotage my car. We spotted him on camera but our surveillance team lost him. No idea where he went."

Mary's eyes widened. "Oh, my."

"It's okay." He winked, then ran his tongue over his teeth. "It means Bingham's panicking, which means we're close to getting our hands on the rest of his money."

"We should ask them to transfer you back to

Washington." She blushed. "I mean, I'm sorry but it seems to me that it's too dangerous for you to be here. You heard what Benji said back at the garage. Bingham won't stop until he kills you."

"With respect, that's a hell no." Lawrence smiled, touched by her concern, the adrenaline of the chase spiking his heart rate once more. "I'm not giving up now, not this close to the trial."

Mary opened the bag of mints and grinned. "Sounds like you're going to need more of these then, sir."

EIGHT

It was after seven o'clock when Mary MacDeaver left the building, her eyes stinging from the hours stuck in air-conditioned air and her back aching from sitting in one of the faux leather conference room chairs.

She paused outside the foyer doors for a moment, acclimatising herself to the evening warmth while traffic passed by languidly, most commuters already home by now.

She had watched with interest while a coordinated effort was made to ascertain where and how Chester Bingham might make another attempt on Lawrence Afflan's life--and how to ensure the man was brought to court in just a few days to end his reign of terror once and for all.

Taking scrupulous notes, she had spent the past six and a half hours listening intently to expert after expert trying to explain to Afflan where their own security had failed, where local law enforcement was still processing the crime scene back at Benji's so-called safe house, and how someone of his calibre had slipped through the cracks to become an assassin for hire.

An urgent recall of all personnel files was also underway, and she shivered despite the heat emanating from the pavement.

Her weapon had been taken away, of course.

All part of the process, they'd said, with Afflan reassuring her that it would only be a matter of days before her full rights were reinstated.

Still… it was unnerving, being unarmed.

Especially now.

She took a step back as a sleek silver saloon car glided past her and crawled to a halt a few yards along the road from where she stood, its tail-lights flaring once before the handbrake was applied.

Mary glanced over her shoulder through the building's glass doors, saw a familiar figure stagger from the elevator, then turned and hurried to the waiting vehicle.

The back door opened for her when she drew closer, cigar smoke wafting out before it was wisped away on the gentle breeze.

She climbed in, the soft purr of the idling engine just audible beyond the plush upholstery and soundproofing.

Chester Bingham removed a cigar from his lips. "Is it done?"

In response, she looked over her shoulder out

the back window to see Lawrence Afflan stumble from the building, closely followed by two security guards, their movements panicked.

A split second later, Afflan clutched his chest and tumbled onto the sidewalk.

Mary swivelled in her seat to face Bingham once more. "It's done."

He hit a button on the upholstered leather armrest beside him. "Go."

As the driver eased the vehicle away, Mary reached into her bag, pulled out the bag of mints and lowered the window.

They fell like tiny hailstones, some tapping the glass on the way to the asphalt before being crushed under the wheels.

The breeze feathered her bangs across her eyes, and she blinked before she buzzed up the glass and looked across at Bingham.

He was all smiles.

"I should've listened to you in the first place," he gushed. "I'm sorry."

"You never were the most patient person. We needed to be subtle." She wrinkled her nose. "Xander and Benji were a mistake. They drew too much attention to you, after all. And they failed."

"No matter now. You're the best, like you always told me." Bingham reached over and patted her hand. "There's a plane waiting for us at a private airfield just north of here. We'll be over the border before they realise what you've done. They'll think he's had a heart attack or something.

And I think you're ready to take over our Pacific interests after today."

Mary beamed. "Thank you."

"We should celebrate," he said, leaning forward to open a mini-bar set into the upholstery. "Here, hold these."

Mary took the crystal glasses from him and waited patiently while he extracted a chilled bottle of champagne from the refrigerator, his eyes scanning the label.

"Good, it's the '92," he said. "The '91 was a crap year."

She smiled indulgently and held the glasses in one hand, reaching into her bag as her phone vibrated.

She ignored the text message.

It could wait.

Mary turned her attention to Bingham while he wrangled the cork free, then held out the glasses. "Not too much for me, I have to drive later."

"Indulge me, then," he said, filling his to the brim before placing the bottle on the floor beside him. "This has been worth the wait."

"And the fee, I hope," she said, clinking her glass against his.

"Of course." He smiled, then took a swig. "I knew you'd be worth it. Your reputation preceded you, even for someone relatively new to this."

She inclined her head in agreement and took a delicate sip before easing back into the luxurious seat.

"Drink up," he said, refilling his glass. "You can relax now."

"Not yet. Like I said, I'm driving later."

Bingham didn't respond.

Instead, he frowned, then coughed.

Then coughed again, slapping his hand against his chest.

"Bubbles…" he managed.

Mary smiled. "Not the bubbles."

Confusion clouded his eyes, then fear.

"You…"

He tumbled forward, crumpling onto the floor beside the half-empty champagne bottle, his glass rolling to her feet.

She pressed the intercom. "Stop the car."

Picking up the glass and dropping it into her bag, she reached under Bingham's jacket, pulled out a snub-nosed revolver, then opened the back door and walked around to the driver's side.

She opened the door and shot the driver between the eyes in one smooth movement.

It took her nearly a minute to drag his cumbersome body from the vehicle and a thin trickle of sweat covered her brow by the time she was done.

Wiping her forehead with her sleeve, Mary then got behind the wheel, reached up, adjusted the rearview mirror and clipped her seatbelt into place.

Her phone rang, and she gave an exasperated sigh before answering. "Yes?"

"Is it done?"

"It is, yes."

"Where are you?"

"I'm on my way."

"Did anyone see you?"

"Negative." She glanced in the rear view mirror to where Bingham's body slumped across the leather upholstery. "Everything went according to plan. The driver's body is where we agreed. Are you okay?"

Lawrence Afflan chuckled. "No thanks to you. What the hell did you put in that stuff?"

"It was only bicarbonate of soda, nothing more."

"Well, it tasted like shit."

"How did you manage to get away?"

"I waited until Bingham's car was out of sight, then told the security team I was okay. The Director told me to take the rest of the week off, and for the first time in my life, I took his advice. With any luck, they won't know what I've done for a day or so."

"What about the money?"

"All transferred out to the family account in the Caymans. It cleared ten minutes ago."

Mary smiled, and then started the engine. "I'm fifteen minutes away."

"Good. We're at the airfield waiting. We should be over the border in forty minutes," said Afflan. "And congratulations, although I wouldn't have minded seeing Bingham's face when he realised he'd been double-crossed. You did a great job, kid."

Mary smiled then pressed her toe to the accelerator.

"You trained me well, pop."

THE END

ABOUT THE AUTHOR

Rachel Amphlett is a USA Today bestselling author of crime fiction and spy thrillers, many of which have been translated worldwide.

Her novels are available in eBook, print, and audiobook formats from libraries and retailers as well as her website shop.

A keen traveller, Rachel has both Australian and British citizenship.

Find out more about Rachel's books at: www.rachelamphlett.com.